Dames In The Atomic Age

written by
CHRISTOPHER RYDER
art by MARC SANDRONI

AN ART OF FICTION BOOK
Published by THE ART OF FICTION, LLC

for my mother
through whom I discovered my love of cheesy rubber science monsters
-C.R.

Inks by Mike Vosburg
Colors by Paul Little
Letters and Design by Tony Fleecs
Cover by Ragnar
Edited by Art of Fiction

With Additional Artwork by
Andy Suriano (p. 11)
Tony Fleecs (p. 23, 24)
Tone Rodriguez, Mark Dos Santos, Steve Downer (p. 38, 39)
Brad Rader, Rahsan Ekedal, Paul Little (p. 53)
Chris Moreno (p. 54, 55, 57)

Special Thanks to Heidi Ryder, Rob and Shannon Ryder,
Josh Fialkov, Jerry Pyle, James Renfroe, Melanie Burgess,
Chris Arundel, Michael O'Rourke and Rob Levin.

Art Of Fiction, LLC
1930 West Olive Avenue
Burbank, CA 91506-2438

ISBN 978-1-937048-08-2

Printed in the United States of America

I'VE ALWAYS LOVED THURSDAYS, EVER SINCE I WAS LITTLE. ALL THE OTHER KIDS, THEY LOVED SATURDAY, BUT NOT ME.

I ALWAYS LOVED THURSDAY.

THURSDAY NIGHT WAS FIGHT NIGHT.

THE NIGHT MY DAD AND UNCLE WOULD TAKE ME TO THE OLYMPIC TO WATCH THE BOUTS.

THE OLYMPIC PRESENTS THURSDAY NIGHT FIGHTS

DOORS at 6:30

LOCAL SENSATION
JULIO
LORDS
VS.
HEAVYWEIGHT GARGANTUAN
WINSTON "THE ECLIPSE"
JOHNSON

Plus
3 LIGHT-
WEIGHT
BOUTS

The Los Angeles Horn

NEW LEADS IN DAHLIA CASE
SPARK WIDER SEARCH

NEW DODGER
DOOGAN!

THE BEST DAMN NIGHT OF THE WEEK.

YAAAAAAHHHHHHHH!

I HEAR THE MUFFLED CHEERS OF THE CROWD FROM INSIDE THE OLYMPIC. I HOPE THEY'RE CHEERING FOR WINSTON...

...BUT SOMEHOW I DOUBT IT.

WINSTON'S MADE A CAREER OUT OF TAKING IT ON THE CHIN.

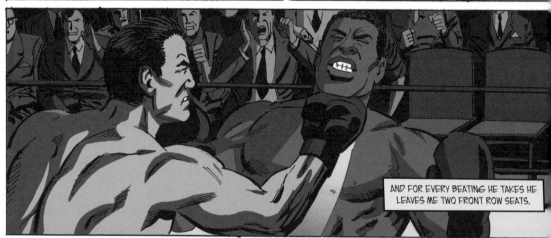

AND FOR EVERY BEATING HE TAKES HE LEAVES ME TWO FRONT ROW SEATS.

A THURSDAY NIGHT GIFT FROM MY MAN IN THE RING.

TONIGHT THERE'S ONE SEAT FOR ME...

...AND ONE SEAT FOR MADDY, THE DAME HIDING BEHIND THE WASTE CANS.

I WAS HIRED TO FIND OUT IF SHE WAS TWO-TIMING HER HUSBAND.

SOME GOVERNMENT FUNDED SCIENTIST FROM D.C.

TURNS OUT SHE WAS...

...WITH WINSTON.

MY CLOSEST FRIEND SLEEPING WITH MY CLIENT'S GIRL.

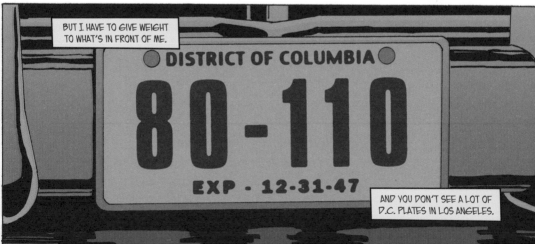

FIZZZARRRRRRRPPPSHHH!

SINCE WHEN COULD THE DAMN RUSSIANS SHOOT LIGHTNING?!

NOSSTAR UPPTORRA.

I'VE GOTTEN INTO MY FAIR NUMBER OF SCRAPES.

ANGRY LOVERS, MOSTLY.

PEOPLE WHO AREN'T HAPPY THAT I'M LOOKING INTO THEIR LIVES.

I'M USED TO CROWBARS AND TIRE IRONS. MAYBE THE OCCASIONAL RUSTY PISTOL.

SKYARR BA RAHKT!

BUT THIS... I DON'T EVEN KNOW WHAT THE HELL THIS IS...

BANG!

YAAAAAAHHHHHHHHHH!

THE CROWD NOISE FROM INSIDE IS LOUD ENOUGH TO MASK THE GUNSHOT.

SADLY, THEY WOULD NEVER CHEER THAT LOUD FOR WINSTON...

...BUT HE'S NOT THE ONE I'M WORRIED ABOUT RIGHT NOW.

WINSTON WILL BE FINE. HE HAS HIS TRAINERS.

ALL WE HAVE IS A DEAD RUSSIAN...

...AND HIS LIGHTNING-SHOOTING REVOLVER.

DAMES

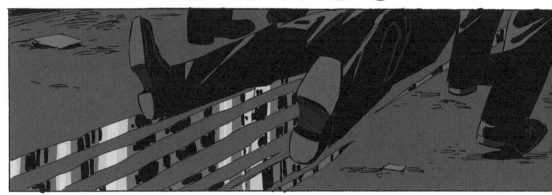

IN THE

ATOMIC AGE

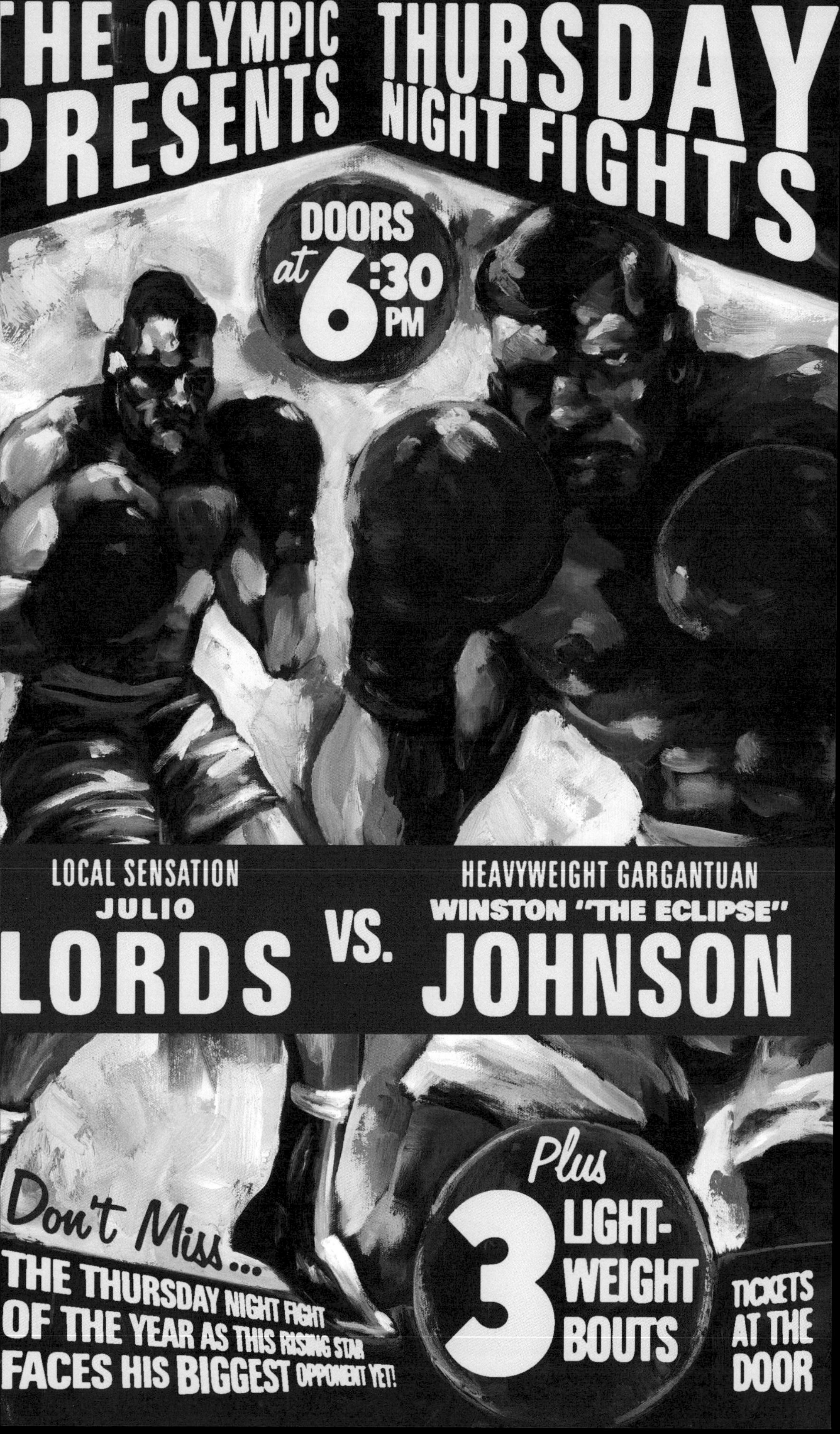

THE OLYMPIC PRESENTS THURSDAY NIGHT FIGHTS

DOORS at 6:30 PM

LOCAL SENSATION
JULIO
LORDS VS.

HEAVYWEIGHT GARGANTUAN
WINSTON "THE ECLIPSE"
JOHNSON

Don't Miss...
THE THURSDAY NIGHT FIGHT
OF THE YEAR AS THIS RISING STAR
FACES HIS BIGGEST OPPONENT YET!

Plus
3 LIGHT-WEIGHT BOUTS

TICKETS AT THE DOOR

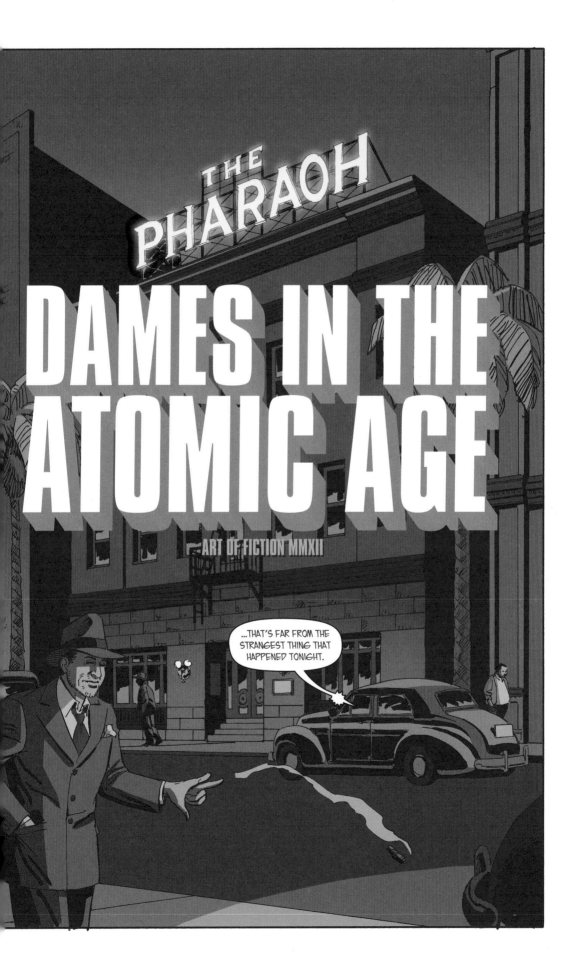

THE PHARAOH BUILDING USED TO HOLD THE KEYS TO THE HOLLYWOOD DREAM.

100
For Rent
104
For R nt
106

200
McCabe Services
204
McCabe Se vices
206
McCabe Services

NOW IT'S ONLY TENANT IS MY EMPLOYER, MCCABE SERVICES

'SERVICES' BEING A FANCY WAY OF SAYING INVESTIGATORS.

I GET HIRED TO FIND PEOPL WHO HAVE GONE MISSING...

...WHETHER THEY WANT TO BE FOUND OR NOT.

COME ON, WINSTON. I NEED TO SHOW YOU SOMETHING.

...AND ONLY FIND WHEN THE BODY WASHES UP UNDER THE SANTA MONICA PIER.

LET'S CONSIDER AN... "CHECKED

NORMALLY WINSTON WOULD NEVER LET RAT GET TO HIM LIKE THAT, BUT HE'S PRETTY WORKED UP TONIGHT.

GETTING BEAT UP IN FRONT OF AN AREN... FULL OF PEOPLE WILL DO THAT TO A MA...

THOUGH I SUSPECT THAT THIS IS ALL ABOUT THE GIRL.

WHAT THE HELL IS THAT?

WATCH.

FIZZZZZZZ.

WINSTON DOESN'T SAY ANYTHING ELSE.

I DON'T EXPECT HIM TO.

HE'S TENSE, FOCUSED...

...THE WAY HE USED TO GET BEFORE A FIGHT.

BACK BEFORE THE PROMOTERS AND MONEY MEN BROKE HIM.

BACK WHEN IT ALL MEANT SOMETHING TO HIM.

NOW THIS DAME MEANS SOMETHING TO HIM...

DODGER DOOGAN, JR. DICK by E.P. Grimfield

DODGER DOOGAN, JR. DICK by E.P. Grimfield

DODGER DOOGAN, JR. DICK by E.P. Grimfield

I SHOULDA KNOWN BETTER THAN TO LET MY GUARD DOWN IN THIS NEIGHBORHOOD.

YER PLAYING A BIT OUTTA YER LEAGUE HERE, DOOGAN.

MICKEY O'ROURKE AND HIS GOONS. PASTE EATERS WHO HANG OUT ON THE CORNER LOOKING FOR TROUBLE.

WHAT DO YOU KNOW ABOUT THE BLACK DOLLY, O'ROURKE?

I DONE TOLD YE ONCE...

...KEEP YER NOSE OUTTA THE DOLLYAAAAHHHHHHHH!

IT WOULD TAKE A FOOLISH FELLOW TO THINK THAT THEIR BEING HERE IS A COINCIDENCE.

LET'S TRY THIS AGAIN...

LUCKY FOR ME, I'M NO FOOL. I ALSO KNOW BETTER THAN TO WADE INTO THE DEEP END WITHOUT A LIFE PRESERVER.

DODGER DOOGAN, JR. DICK by E.P. Grimfield

TYPICALLY I'M NOT THE KIND OF GUY TO PULL A SHOOTER ON THE STREET.

IS ONE OF YOU GONNA TELL ME WHAT YOU HAD TO GAIN BY TAKING LIZZY SMALL'S DOLLY, OR DO I HAVE TO START SLINGING SLUGS?

BUT DESPERATE TIMES CALL FOR UNCOMMON REACTIONS...

THEY RIPPED THE DOLLY UP GOOD, THEY DID, BUT THEY DINT STEAL IT FROM NO GIRL.

...AND YOU CAN USUALLY TRUST A MAN TO TELL THE TRUTH WHEN HE'S STARING DOWN A BARREL.

SHE GAVE IT TO EM ALL ON HER OWN.

THAT'S RIGHT...

SEEMS THAT'S THE ONLY THING YOU CAN TRUST.

...AND I'D HAVE A BRAND NEW DOLLY BY NOW IF TH GIANT LUG HADN'T SEEN US.

DODGER DOOGAN, JR. DICK by E.P. Grimfield

I SHOULD HAVE KNOWN BETTER THAT TO LISTEN TO A CRYING DAME.

WHAT'S YOUR GAME, LIZZY?

USUALLY MY INSTINCTS ARE GOOD, BUT THOSE TEARS...

I WAS TIRED OF THE BLACK DOLLY AND I WANTED A NEW ONE, BUT DADDY SAID NO.

...IT'S LIKE THEY'RE MADE TO CLOUD A GUY'S THINKING.

HE SAID I LOSE THEM TOO OFTEN, AND WON'T BUY ME ANY MORE.

A THIMBLE FULL OF TEARS AND TH CAN PLAY YOU LIKE A FIDD

BUT IF YOU TOLD HIM SOMEONE TOOK IT, HE HAVE NO CHOICE.

EVERYONE KNOWS THA DODGER DOOG ALWAYS TELL THE TRUTH.

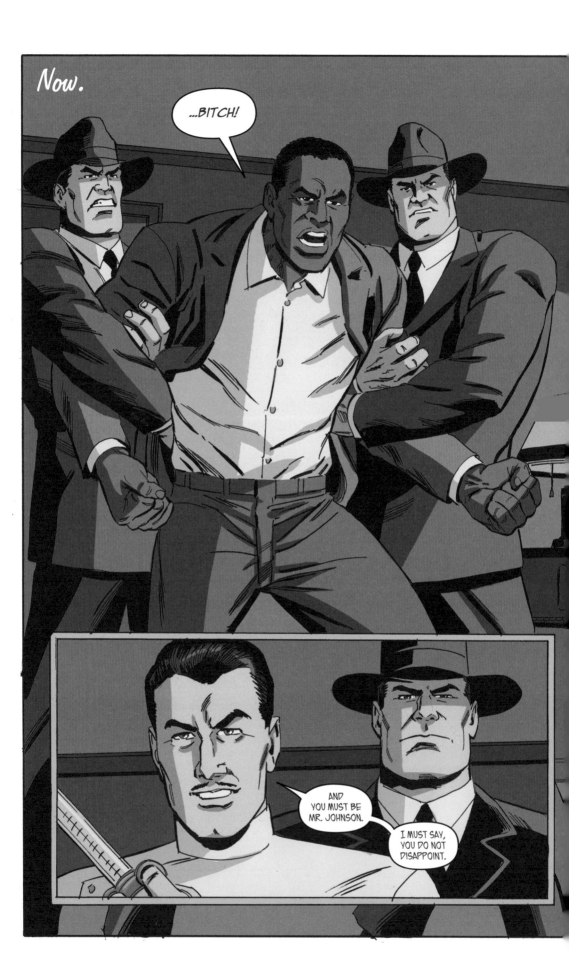

YOUR COMPANY HAS LIVED UP TO ITS REPUTATION, MR. FISCH.

CAVORTING WITH THOSE YOU WERE HIRED TO LOCATE, HOWEVER...

...THAT'S JUST NOT VERY PROFESSIONAL.

I CAN SEE WHY YOU CHOSE THIS ONE, DARLING. QUITE THE SPECIMEN.

YOU SON OF A...

OOOUF!

CALM YOURSELF, SIR. EVEN A BRUTE LIKE YOU CAN SHOW SOME MANNERS.

ACTUALLY DOCTOR, HE'S NOT A BRUTE...

...HE'S A FIGHTER!

THERE'S A LOT OF THINGS I SHOULD BE FOCUSED ON RIGHT NOW.

MY LAND LADY IS ON THE FLOOR, POSSIBLY DEAD.

SOME CRAZY FRANKENSTEIN HAS MY BEST FRIEND'S GIRL BY THE NECK.

SUBDUE THEM, GENTLEMEN, AND MEET ME IN THE DESERT!

THE LAST TIME I SAW THESE COMMIES THEY SHOT LIGHTNING AT ME.

NOSH BLIGARR!

BUT ALL I CAN ACTUALLY THINK IS...

I WATCHED ONE OF THEM DIE.

NOSH BLIGARR!

I SAW ONE OF THESE DUPLICATE RED BASTARDS TAKE A SLUG.

A BULLET, RIGHT TO THE FOREHEAD.

AND NOW HE'S BACK.

KAGRAAASCI

SKREEEEEEEE

SKYARR BA RAHKT!

DURRSTCH.

SCHRUUUU

Dames

in the

Atomic Age

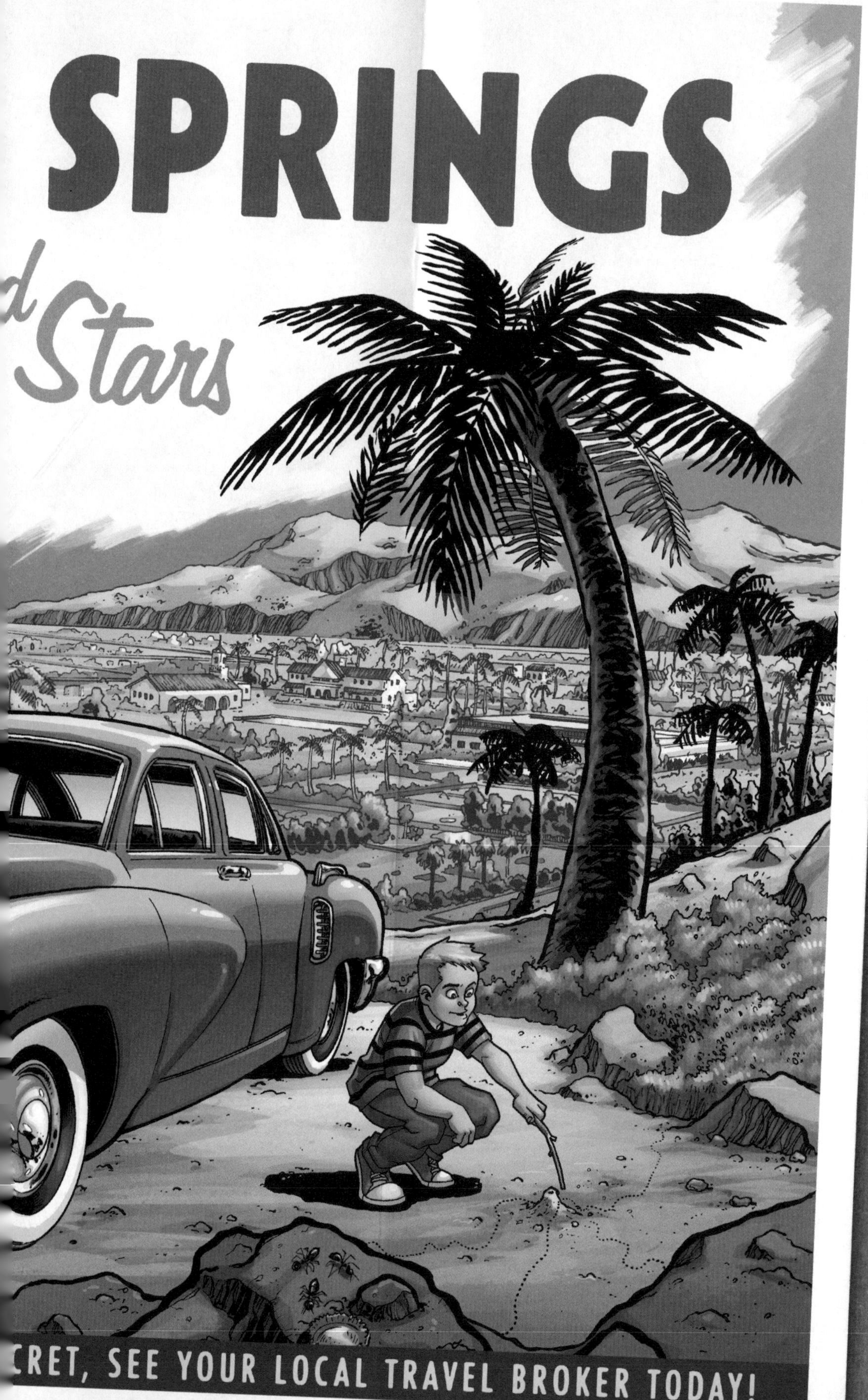
SPRINGS
d Stars
CRET, SEE YOUR LOCAL TRAVEL BROKER TODAY!

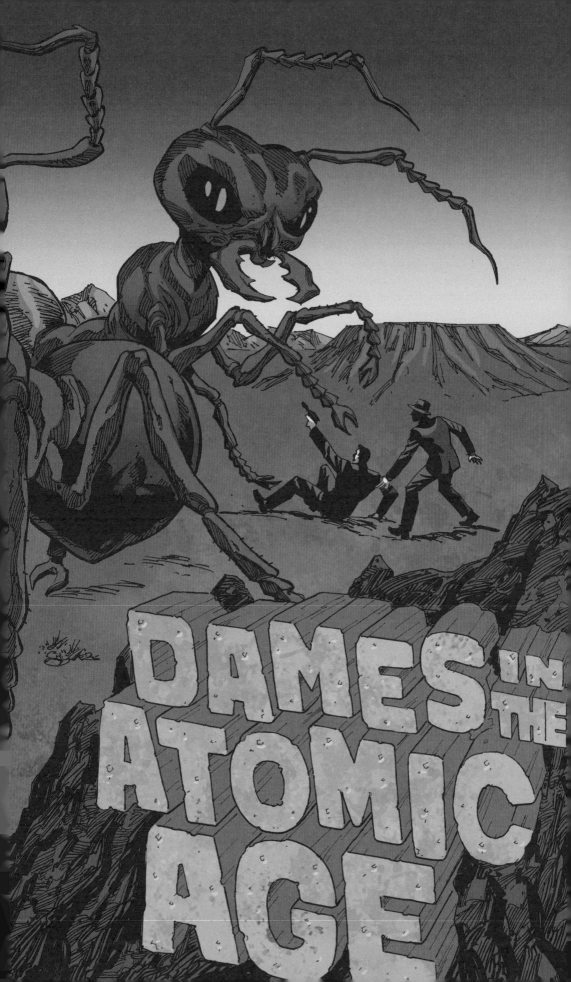

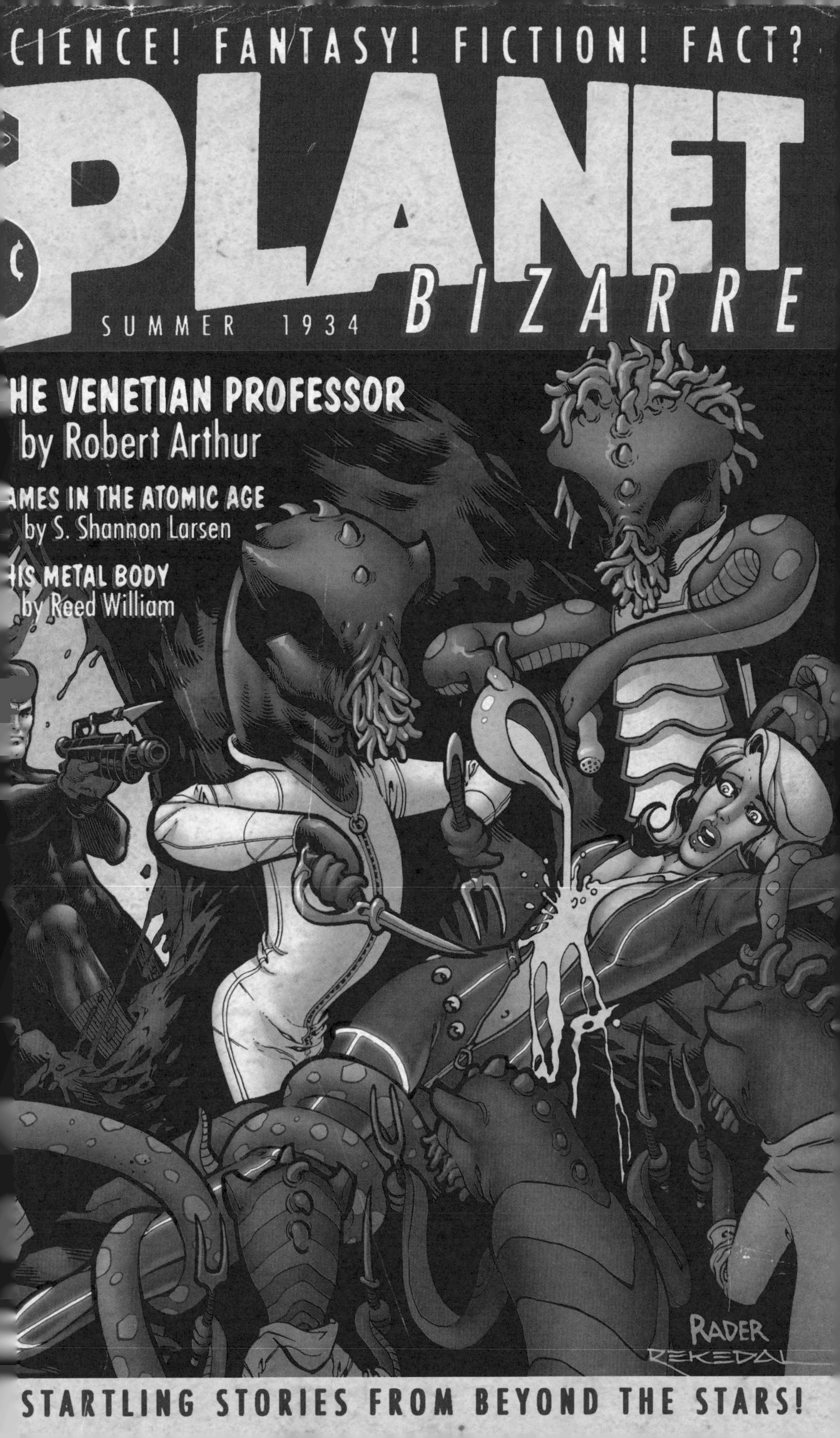

SCIENCE! FANTASY! FICTION! FACT?

PLANET
BIZARRE

SUMMER 1934

THE VENETIAN PROFESSOR
by Robert Arthur

GAMES IN THE ATOMIC AGE
by S. Shannon Larsen

HIS METAL BODY
by Reed William

RADER
REKEDAL

STARTLING STORIES FROM BEYOND THE STARS!

DAMES IN THE ATOMIC AGE

I SHOULD HAVE STAYED AT THE BONFIRE. IT WAS OUR FINAL NIGHT OF PREP SCHOOL AND THE WHOLE CLASS HAD COME OUT TO OLD MAN PYLE'S FIELD. JAMES JIMBLES EVEN SWIPED SOME OF HIS DADDY'S HOOCH. I SHOULD HAVE JUST STAYED AND DRANK, BUT WHEN I SAW JEFFREY SCOTT, MY BEST FRIEND SINCE WE WERE FIVE, DISAPPEAR INTO THE WOODS WITH HEIDI LINNETTE, MY CURIOSITY WAS TOO GREAT TO IGNORE.

I DIDN'T THINK. I JUST RAN INTO THE BLINDING LIGHT, DIVING TO PULL MY FRIEND BACK TO THE GROUND.

BUT BEFORE I COULD REGRET IT, I WAS SWEPT WEIGHTLESSLY TOWARDS THE SKY. PULLED UPWARDS WITHOUT CONTROL.... AND THEN EVERYTHING JUST WENT BLACK.

WHEN I FINALLY CAME TO I WAS DISORIENTATED... I THOUGHT I WAS BACK IN MY POP'S WAREHOUSE, BUT THEN I SAW ALL THOSE FLASHING LIGHTS...

...AND JEFFREY LYING THERE IN THE MIDDLE OF THE ROOM...

STOP, JEFFREY! WE DON'T KNOW WHAT'S OUT THERE!

EVER SINCE WE WERE KIDS JEFFREY HAS BEEN QUICK TO ACT... HE'S A DO-ER, NOT A THINKER, AND BEFORE I KNEW IT HE WAS ON HIS FEET AND RUNNING FOR THE DOOR...

AND ONCE HE HEARD HEIDI SCREAM, THERE WAS NO HOLDING HIM BACK.

AAAAAAHHHHHHH!!

I'VE ALWAYS BEEN MORE CAUTIOUS, MORE TIMID... I LIKE TO PLAN AHEAD...

AAAAAAHHHHHHH!!

...BUT ONCE JEFFREY IS IN MOTION IT'S HARD TO GET HIM TO STOP.

UNLESS THERE'S SOMETHING THERE READY TO STOP HIM.

WINSTON! PUT THAT BOOK DOWN, KID.

WHAT... HOW...

TWO EXCELLENT QUESTIONS, MR. JOHNSON.

SHHHHHKACHUUUNK

DO YOU RECALL THAT "AIR RAID" INCIDENT BACK IN THE WINTER OF 1942?

THE PAPERS DUBBED IT "THE BATTLE OF LOS ANGELES." UNIDENTIFIED CRAFT IN THE SKY. THE CITY BLACKED OUT AS ANTI-AIRCRAFT SHELLS BURST OVERHEAD.

THE GOVERNMENT WAS QUICK TO BLAME THE JAPS, BUT IN TRUTH, WE DID SHOOT SOMETHING OUT OF THE SKY THAT NIGHT...

...AND WE'VE SPENT THE PAST 5 YEARS ESTABLISHING COMMUNICATION, AND, ULTIMATELY, THE ADAPTATION OF WHAT WE SHOT DOWN.

WIZZZZHHHHH

WHICH BRINGS US TO THE "HOW" OF MR. JOHNSON'S QUESTION.

THROUGH THIS DEVICE I AM ABLE TO SIPHON HUMAN CELLULAR MATERIAL AND USE IT TO RESHAPE THE UNIQUE PHYSIOLOGY OF OUR FOREIGN FRIENDS.

SADLY, IT HAS A DESTRUCTIVE EFFECT ON THE "DONOR'S" BODY, AND THIS ONE IS READY TO BE REPLACED.

WIZZZZHHHHHH

AND THAT, MY DEAR WINSTON, IS THE REASON WE NEED YOU.

MADDY?

I'M VERY SORRY, DARLING. I TRULY AM. YOU ACTUALLY GOT INTO MY HEAD. MADE ME FORGET MY PRIORITIES.

MADDY, WHAT ARE YOU TALKING ABOUT?

DON'T YOU SEE, MR. JOHNSON?

MADELINE HAS HAND PICKED YOU TO BE THE NEXT CELLULAR BLUEPRINT FOR OUR ALIEN COMPANIONS!

WHAT?! NO!

LET ANDREW GO AND I'LL COME WITHOUT A FIGHT.

JUST LET ANDREW GO.

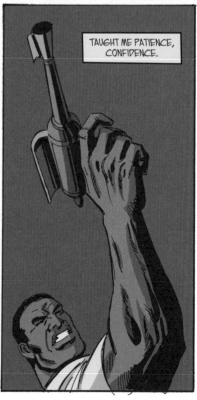

WE CONVINCED OURSELVES THAT COACH'S MANTRA WAS TRUE...

ZAFEE CESUR AITTIR.

...THAT FORTUNE FAVORS THE BRAVE.

NOOOOOOOOO!

WINSTON'S BEEN PUSHED AROUND MOST OF HIS LIFE.

UNDERESTIMATED.

UNDER APPRECIATED.

BY TRAINERS.

BY OPPONENTS.

BY DAMES.

I SUPPOSE THAT'S WHY WE ALWAYS GOT ON SO WELL.

WE'RE BOTH MISFITS IN OUR OWN WAY.

SIZZZARRRRRRPPP!

PEOPLE COULD NEVER SEE PAST HIS EXTERIOR...

PSSSHHHHHHHHHH

...AND THEY NEVER SAW ME MUCH AT ALL.

SO WE TOOK THAT AND CONSTRUCTED THE LIVES THAT MADE THE MOST SENSE IN THIS WORLD.

THE PALOOKA AND THE DICK.

BUT IN LIGHT OF RECENT EVENTS, I CAN'T HELP BUT WONDER...

YOU GOING TO BE OK?

NO.

WHAT DO WE BECOME NOW THAT THE WORLD HAS STOPPED MAKING SENSE?

NOT EVEN A LITTLE.

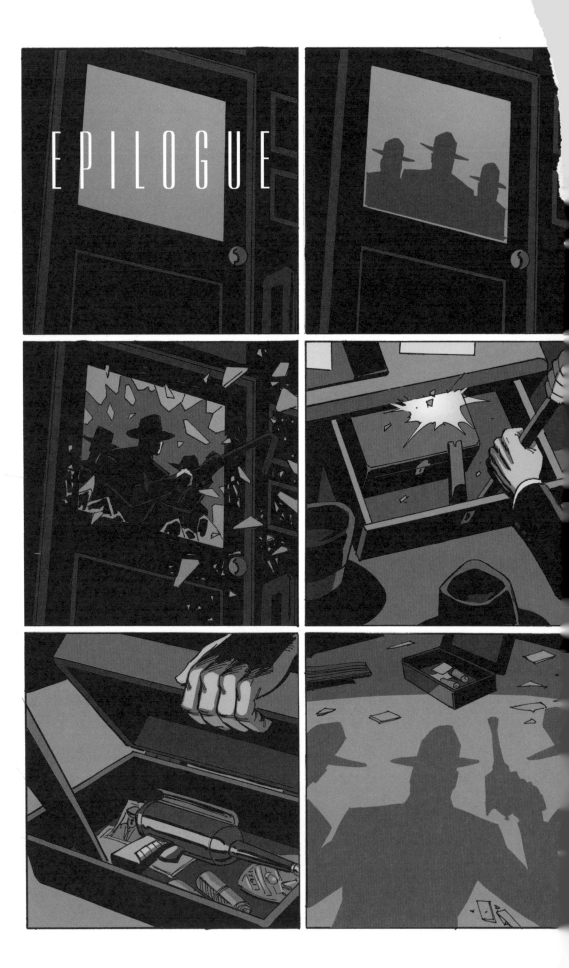

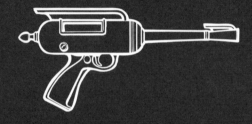

THE ART OF FICTION, U.S.A.

1930 W OLIVE AVE
BURBANK, CA 91506-2438

HOUSE OF SECRETS

Comics and Toys

1930 WEST OLIVE AVE
BURBANK, CA 91506
(818) 562-1900

ARTOFFICTION.COM/HOUSEOFSECRETS